DEADWOOD HALL

Book 1
of the Oozing Magic series

Linda Jones

Illustrated by
David Hailwood

This First Edition of Deadwood Hall published in Great Britain in 2018 by Linda Jones Bavoom Publishing

www.facebook.com/LindaJonesukAuthor/

Cover design and illustrations by
David Hailwood

ISBN: 978-1-9993248-0-3

Dedication

For
Michelle and Dylan

Contents

Acknowledgements

Thank you to Michelle Beck for taking the time and energy to read and encourage.

To the Writing group at the Regent's Hotel in Doncaster, after six years they are still as creative and supportive as ever.

And to the brilliantly talented David Hailwood, illustrator/writer extraordinaire, zany, patient and very, very funny!

1

Almost Christmas

Dylan watched the icy flakes as they swirled past the car window. Caught by the wind, it was like the snow had transformed into huge beasts, their mouths opening wide in a silent howl. He nudged his sister, hard. 'Wow. Look outside. It's like we're being chased by massive snow monsters!'

'Stop elbowing me,' Emily complained. 'Mum, tell him?'

The short journey to their grandfather's house had already taken three times longer than usual. The arguments had started almost as soon as the car engine had roared into life.

'Both of you just be quiet,' said their mother. 'Or I'll ask Dad to drop you off at your Aunty Greta's!'

The threat made nine-year-old Dylan Beaumont squirm in his seat. 'Urgh, she's ancient and she smells of cats.'

'I'm just glad we haven't got far to go,' said their father. 'This snow is getting worse by the second.' The wipers were skating across the icy windscreen in a frantic attempt to keep up with the fast-falling flakes.

'Did you pack the sleds, Mum?' Emily asked. She was trying to ignore Dylan and his silly yellow bobble hat.

'They're in the boot,' her mother answered. 'I just hope this weather eases off a little. It's hard to see anything with this snow swirling around.'

'It would be way cool if we got stuck and had to be rescued,' said Dylan. He pushed his glasses back up his nose and wished the snow would fall even harder.

'No, it wouldn't,' Emily said, rolling her eyes. 'It would be freezing cold, and it could take ages for someone to reach us. Isn't that right, Dad?'

'We aren't going to be stranded,' said their father. 'Ten minutes and we'll be there.'

Dylan made a point of ignoring his boring sister. She was eleven and never wanted to play or do anything fun anymore. He was going to be stuck at his grandfather's house with just his miserable sister and no friends to play with; not even their grandfather would be there because he had to go away for a few days. Christmas was going to be awful!

He pulled his Transformer truck from his bag and imagined an alien spacecraft preparing to attack. '*Zoom*, blast 'em from the sky...*Emergency landing!*' The truck flew from his fingers and landed with a thump on Emily's leg.

She flung it back at him in irritation. 'Next time I'll throw it outside!' But, as usual, he ignored her. 'I warned you,' she said, snatching up the truck from her lap. As she wound down her window a couple of inches, a noisy blast of cold air swept inside. With it came the oddest smell, of dirty water and musty socks.

Emily raised the truck to the gap, turned to her brother, and grinned.

But Dylan's eyes had bulged wide open in horror. Clinging to the outside of her window was a hideous snake-like creature, its huge purplish face squashed tightly against the glass. Jagged teeth bared, it was snapping and biting, trying to tear its way into the car.

‘No! No, please don’t,’ he begged, unable to draw his eyes away from the terrifying sight.

Emily’s grin widened. ‘You’ll have to try harder than that.’

‘Close that window now,’ their mother ordered, without bothering to look around.

‘Did...did you see that...that *thing*?’ Dylan pointed to where the creature had been only seconds before. ‘Outside, there was some sort of ice monster.’

‘Like I’m that stupid,’ said Emily and started to read her book, refusing to talk to him.

Dylan twisted in his seat to look anxiously out through the rear window. Weird shapes seemed to dance in the thick, driving snow, but it was impossible to see anything properly. He shivered. He was sure he hadn’t imagined it. Those teeth had been far too scary to be just snowflakes playing tricks.

‘At last,’ said his father as the car turned left onto a long gravel driveway. ‘I just hope this clears up by Saturday or your grandfather won’t be going anywhere.’

‘It has to,’ said Emily. ‘I’ve got to go to Sarah’s party on Monday or she’ll never speak to me again, ever!’

When the car stopped, the first thing Dylan did was to trudge around to Emily’s door. He swept off the flakes that had landed and stared at the glistening blue paintwork. There wasn’t a single scratch or mark anywhere in sight. Perhaps it had been the snow playing tricks after all

2

The Party

Their grandfather lived in a large and very unusual house, nothing at all like the tiny terraced house Dylan lived in. On the roof sat a line of higgledy-piggledy chimney pots that squatted like funny old men. Inside was an amazing staircase that wound its way up through the three floors to the dusty attic. If Dylan was feeling brave (and no one was looking) he could kick his leg over the banister at the top and slide really fast, all the way down.

The problem was you could only live in about half of the upstairs because the roof leaked and several of the rooms downstairs were closed off due to the damp. The kitchen was the best room, with the warm Aga and a huge table.

There were plenty of places to hide as well, like the cupboards, which were full of dusty old toys and peculiar objects, some of which glowed with a strange orange hue. Sometimes, when he opened one of the cupboard doors, he was sure he could hear tiny footsteps scurrying away through all the clutter - but it was probably just mice, or at least he hoped so. He really hated rats.

All the cabinets and shelves were lined with odd curios as well. His least favourite was the creepy china doll; she was only the size of an egg cup but had bright red lips, raven black hair and a purple lump on the end of her nose that made her look like a witch. The porcelain model of a bird that sat next to her was very impressive, but even that made Dylan shiver. Its golden plumage was painted the colour of fire and its eyes were such a piercing blue they almost looked alive.

He much preferred the gorilla that sat on a shelf in his grandfather's study. It was the smallest model that Dylan had ever seen, complete with dense dark fur and red eyes that seemed to follow him around the room. It was perfect in every detail.

The best bit of all though had to be the garden. It was full of trees and shaggy bushes, great for making dens; there was even a tree-swing. Up against the back hedge was a large overgrown pond, almost as big as a swimming pool.

Sometimes, when he'd been sailing paper boats or pond dipping, he was sure he could see the weirdest creatures moving around in the murky depths - creatures that suddenly leapt to the surface to drag down his little boat or net.

He was going to keep his toes and fingers well away from that water!

The reason they always went to their grandfather's the week before Christmas was for the party. Every year it was the same; on the evening of the 21st of December, the old house filled with people he didn't recognise, all dressed up in their finest clothes. The downstairs rooms sparkled with decorations.

Apparently, the 'party' was to celebrate the Winter Solstice, the shortest day of the year. Why that was so important Dylan had never found out, and he didn't really care because neither he nor his sister was ever invited. But at least there was the local pantomime to look forward to (their treat), and of course they got to taste all the party food his mum and dad made.

When Dylan opened his curtains on Saturday, the day of the party, he sighed with disappointment. The sky was a clear blue, which meant his grandad would be leaving for the airport after all.

'Do you really have to go, Grandad?' he asked as they sat around the kitchen table for breakfast.

'I'm afraid so,' said his grandad. 'Miss McCrery is very ill and I promised to visit her.'

Dylan had never heard of this Miss McCrery before, so it was very hard to feel sorry for her.

'But it's Christmas, Grandad and you'll miss the party...'

'Enough, Dylan,' his father said. 'I'm taking your grandad to the airport in half an hour, so please don't make this harder than it already is.'

Dylan and Emily stood at the big front door to wave their grandfather off. The tall, grey-haired man had hugged them both hard before hurrying away. As the car disappeared out of sight, Dylan shivered. He was already feeling gloomy. The old house felt empty and sad without him there.

'Let's go out and see if we can build a snow castle,' suggested Emily. 'Mum's busy cooking for the party tonight, so at least we won't get in her way.'

It had snowed heavily during the night. The whole garden was covered in a thick white blanket. 'Bet I can make the best towers,' said Dylan, already cheering up at the suggestion.

'Not a chance, but I bet between us we can make the biggest snow castle ever.'

It was a long time later when Emily stopped to study her brother's latest creation. Around the outer walls of their castle, he had made a neat row of pineapple-shaped trees. 'Did Mum say you could use those?' she asked, eyeing the shining jelly moulds.

'Sort of and they are metal, so it's not like I can break them.' He pushed his glasses up his cold nose. 'Do you want to have a try with the fish one I borrowed?'

By late afternoon their castle was standing several feet high. It was surrounded by a whole forest of pineapple trees, and a moat now filled with fish-shaped mounds.

'Cool,' said their father, admiringly. 'And I won't ask where you found those jelly moulds.' He began to take photographs. 'It's better than a boring old snowman and those turrets are a nice touch.'

After a tea of crispy baked potatoes filled with beans and cheese, they sat in front of the roaring fire toasting crumpets and marshmallows on a long fork. With the Christmas tree lights glittering, the big front room looked spectacular.

'Couldn't we just stay downstairs until everyone arrives?' Dylan pleaded.

'Bedroom,' ordered his mother as the mantle-clock chimed eight. 'You have enough films and games up there to keep you going for a week. Please be good, we don't do this often.'

They were sharing a bedroom again, which they both agreed was rubbish. According to Emily, her brother snored and left his stuff all over the floor. She talked in her sleep and bossed him about, or so Dylan said (Emily had to agree that the last bit was probably true). Sprawled over big cushions on the floor, they sipped juice and watched their favourite films, trying to ignore the increasing noise from down below.

'You want to watch another film?' Dylan asked as the credits began to roll.

'Not really.' Emily sighed, as a particularly loud laugh echoed up through the floorboards.

'We could play with my Transformers?' suggested Dylan, pulling out one of his toy figures.

'As if.' She wandered across to the tall window and gazed out over the moonlit garden. Something small hit her on the cheek and she jumped. Eyes narrowed, she turned to discover Dylan was holding up two fingers, an elastic-band stretched between them. He had another screwed-up missile already loaded, ready to fire. 'You were told not to do that,' she said rubbing at her sore cheek.

'It's only bits of paper and I bet I can shoot them further than you.'

They spent ten minutes or so squashing up paper and catapulting missiles around the room. Dylan even tried one of his Transformers but that was much too big.

'These paper bullets are too light,' he complained. 'There might be something we could use on those shelves out in the hallway.'

'No!' hissed Emily, but he was already opening the bedroom door. 'You'll get into so much trouble.'

'Only if they find out,' he whispered. From downstairs came the sound of music and laughter. ‘And it isn’t like anyone’s going to hear us with that racket going on.’

He pushed aside the ancient maps, carved pieces of bone and some large model cars. It was then he spotted the three small lead figures. ‘What are these doing here?’ he whispered. ‘They're usually in Grandad’s study.’

One was an old-fashioned soldier, wearing a bright red uniform jacket, a gleaming sword hung at his side.

Another wore green camouflage; brown streaks coated his tiny cheeks. The last was dark-skinned, slim and elegant. She had gold bracelets around her ankle and arm and a sandy-coloured cloak that fell in ripples from her shoulders. They were all only three inches high.

'This one should be perfect,' whispered Dylan and picked up the model soldier.

'Put it back. You're going to break it,' warned Emily.

But he wasn't listening. 'Stop being a scaredy cat.'

At the first attempt the soldier's sword got caught in the elastic. The model spun just once, before falling onto his toe with a thump.

'It serves you right!' Emily laughed at him as he yelped and began hopping across the wooden floor.

'I'll turn him around then it'll work.' More determined than ever, Dylan raised his hand, the elastic-band drawn tightly between his fingers. In the distance, the church clock began to strike eleven. The notes were crystal clear in the cold night air.

'Honestly, Dylan, this is a really bad —' Before Emily could finish her sentence, the elastic had twanged. Over and over the soldier spun, faster and faster - heading straight towards the glass of the closed window.

'No!' they cried out together.

Then the strangest thing happened – with a SWISH the window flew up. The soldier spun on and on, out into the moonlit night

3

A Stink In The Night

Now look what you've done,' hissed Emily. 'You are going to be in so much trouble!'

'B-but that was magic,' spluttered Dylan.

'Rubbish. Dad was saying all the window catches are broken,' she insisted. 'And he's going to be furious when he finds out what you did, as will Grandad. Those models are his favourite things.'

'I didn't know it was going to happen like that. I thought it would just fall out.'

'You never listen,' yelled Emily, angry because she knew she would get half the blame.

'Like you never do anything wrong.'

They both heard shoes clumping up the stairs. 'Oh great, now someone's on the way up! Quick...' Emily tugged down the window, and grabbed her brother's hand to pull him to the floor. When the bedroom door opened, they were lying over cushions, innocently watching the TV screen.

'What were you arguing about?' asked their mother.

'Only what film to watch,' Dylan lied. He kept his brown eyes fixed on the flickering screen.

'And where are your glasses?' she asked.

With a groan, he reached over to the bedside cabinet and picked them up. 'Sorry,' he mumbled, fumbling them on.

'I don't want to hear you again, understood?' She bent down to drop a kiss on Dylan's short spiky hair and his sister's curly brown locks. Her own curly hair was caught up in a knot at the back of her head. A sparkling band of jewels kept it in place.

'Yes Mum,' they chorused.

'Staying up late is supposed to be a treat. Here, I've brought you some cake and biscuits for a midnight feast.' Dylan's eyes lit up. The biscuits were his favourite. They had jam in the centre, which meant he could stick his tongue in and lick it out. 'Don't get cold,' his mother warned. She hurried away, the sparkles on her dress flashing like a galaxy of stars.

'That was close,' said Emily, turning off the film.

'Thanks for not telling,' mumbled Dylan. He walked over to the window. The sky was much darker now. The full moon was hardly visible at all.

'We should be able to search for the soldier first thing in the morning, before anyone finds out,' said Emily.

'No we won't,' Dylan groaned. 'It's snowing really hard. He'll be all covered up and I'll never find him.'

'It will serve you right if you miss out on the pantomime or something.' But Emily had a horrible feeling it wouldn't just be her brother who would be in trouble. After all, she was supposed to be keeping an eye on him. 'Well, I'm not going to be grounded for the rest of the holidays, so I suppose we'd better try and get him back tonight. But if I miss out on Sarah's party because of you...'

'Really...You'll help?' Dylan beamed at her.

'Like I could trust you to find it on your own. But no more catapult. You have to promise?' She crossed her arms and frowned.

'I promise,' he said.

They put on their socks, pulling them up over the bottom of their pyjamas. 'Keep your dressing gown on. We'll put our coats over the top,' Emily said. 'And where are your glasses?'

He'd taken them off again as soon as his mother had left the room.

Reluctantly, Dylan did as she said. Picking up a couple of biscuits, he pushed them into his dressing gown pocket for later.

There was a lot of noise from the party downstairs, so it was easy to slip along to the small rear staircase that no one ever used. As they crept down the narrow steps, Dylan ducked away from the dusty cobwebs dangling from the shadowy corners. He tried really hard not to think about what lived in the holes in the skirting boards and whether they had sharp teeth. Near the back door their wellington boots stood waiting. Their coats and Dylan's bobble hat hung from a peg, but their gloves were still too wet to wear.

'Here goes,' whispered Emily and unlocked the door.

It was like walking out into a different world. Snow crunched under their boots; it sounded so much louder at night. Dylan pulled down his hat over his ears and took a long deep breath. The air seemed to crackle in his lungs, it was so cold.

Emily pointed to the left. 'If we go that way, we should be right under our bedroom. We can start searching from there.'

'I hope no one checks our room,' whispered Dylan. He plunged his hands deep into his coat pockets. His fingers and toes were already tingling with the cold.

'They're too busy having a good time,' said Emily. 'Wish our gloves had been dry, my hands are freezing.'

As soon as they were safely past the window, they began searching. The light streaming from the windows helped, but as they walked further into the garden it became far more difficult to see anything clearly.

'A torch would've been useful,' grumbled Dylan.

'Someone would've spotted the light,' Emily whispered back. 'You look to the right and I'll look left. If we keep a few feet apart we'll find him.'

They were almost up to the tree swing when they both heard a loud rustling. Emily spun around, her nose twitching. 'Can you smell that?' she whispered, wrinkling her nose in disgust. 'Yuck, it really stinks.'

'It must be a fox. Their droppings can smell pretty bad.' Dylan pushed a cold hand inside to his dressing gown pocket, digging around for the biscuits.

'What are you talking about?' muttered Emily.

'Well, that's what Grandad told me.' Dylan took a bite of a biscuit, his teeth chattering in the cold, and pushed the rest into his coat pocket for later.

'Let's just get up to the pond, then we'll walk back and try again,' said Emily. 'I thought we'd have found him by now.'

By the time Dylan had reached the pond, he was beginning to feel desperate. At least the snow had stopped for now and there was even a glimpse of moonlight. Without much hope, he turned to walk back towards the snow castle, but his glasses had misted up and he could hardly see a thing. He rubbed the lenses clear and then let out a hoot of delight.

Just a few yards away something small and bright red was sticking out of a turret of the snow castle.

'Emily I found him!' Dylan tried to hurry through the thick snow. It wasn't until he had almost reached the castle that he realised his sister hadn't answered. 'Emily?' he called again. He looked right, left and twisted all around.

His sister wasn't anywhere to be seen.

4

Soldier Soldier

Dylan jumped from one foot to the other, trying to stay warm. 'Stop messing about. It's too cold to start hiding.' *And spooky* he thought, as he waited for her to answer. *I bet she's getting her own back and has gone home without me...*

But when he looked, all he could see were the two sets of footprints leading from the house. 'Emily, please…I'm really, really sorry about the catapult!'

'You'd better dig me out if you want to find her...' said a small, tinny voice.

Startled, Dylan looked around, but couldn't see anyone. It didn't sound a bit like his sister. 'Who's there? Emily? Stop playing. It isn't funny anymore.'

'Down here, human. We don't have much time. Pull me out!' The voice was definitely coming from that snow castle.

'No chance!' Dylan tried to run but his foot slipped on an icy patch. He hit the floor with a *SMACK*, and slid on his backside, legs and arms flapping madly. There was a final *FLUMP* as his head butted against the side of the castle.

Dylan wiped the frozen snow from his eyes and couldn't believe what he was seeing. That lead soldier was scooping away snow with tiny hands, trying to free himself.

'Are you just going to sit and watch me?' called the soldier. 'If we don't get a move on, it will be too late.' The tiny voice sounded as if it was coming from miles away.

'Y-y-you can't be real,' gasped Dylan, still too shocked to move.

'It's Midwinter's Night, young human, when there's powerful magic abroad. They've taken her to the Deadwood Hall. We've less than an hour to rescue her. Are you listening?'

'B-but —' stuttered Dylan.

'Dig me out,' insisted the soldier.

It was like being in a dream. Maybe he was? Only this dream had made his hands freezing cold and he couldn't feel the tip of his nose. The icy snow was wet as his trembling fingers dug in. 'Y-you won't hurt me will you?' Dylan asked.

'What, like sling you from a piece of elastic, do you mean?' said the soldier.

Dylan's cold cheeks were now burning red-hot. 'Sorry,' he mumbled.

'Humph...Just hurry it up. If the clock chimes twelve and we haven't got her home, then the Whivick queen wins.'

Dylan dug away the last of the snow and the small soldier sprang out, up onto his outstretched hand. The soldier pulled something shiny from inside his red jacket. Dylan squinted and realised it was a tiny horn.

'Walk to that ash tree and then put me down. Come on human, this isn't a game!'

'But —'

'We'll argue about it after. *Move!*' Dylan turned and walked the few paces to the tree. 'Just here is fine,' shouted the soldier. Dylan lowered him to the ground and was just about to ask what would happen next, when —

'TA-RAAH!' A blast of noise rang out as the soldier blew hard on the shiny instrument.

Dylan's world began to spin and swirl, faster and faster. Everything was all muddled up like a gigantic Kaleidoscope. '*Heeelp!'* he cried as his legs and arms jerked uncontrollably; it felt like his head was going to explode. Now he was falling, down, down into something white and very cold. *Thump*! He lay for a long moment, too scared to open his eyes. When he did, there was a pair of piercing green eyes staring down at him. His father? No, definitely wasn't his dad.

'Give me your hand, human,' said a deep voice.

'Wow...you've grown,' said Dylan.

The soldier laughed and held out a hand. 'It's the other way around. Up, lad and follow me to the oak.'

With a swift tug, Dylan was up on his feet. Everything was gigantic. He couldn't see to the top of the tree. As they hurried along, he almost tripped over an acorn that was half buried in the snow. It was so big he could have sat on it.

Above their heads, soft wings swept through the air.

'Quickly!' warned the soldier. 'We need to get to the oak and down into the tunnels.' He drew out his sword, looking anxiously up at the star-spangled sky.

'What was that?' whispered Dylan.

'An Owl. It thinks we're his supper and I haven't got time to explain otherwise.'

It was difficult to walk. Dylan's feet kept sliding out from under him; the mounds of snow and large stones made it even harder. 'It's just a dream,' he muttered as he staggered on. 'I'll wake up in a bit.' But the cold just kept getting colder and the night scarier.

'It's over here.' The soldier caught his hand, pulling Dylan closer to the broad trunk. 'Are you ready?' asked the soldier, sounding grim.

'No,' said Dylan, but he knew it wouldn't make any difference.

With a *SWISH* the soldier raised the glinting sword, then *CRACK*! He struck the tree with all his might. There was a faint shimmer of green. Creaking and groaning, an arched opening began to appear, dimly at first, but gradually growing brighter.

‘Stay close, human,’ whispered the soldier. ‘The Whivicks will have posted lookouts and they are very partial to a tasty young human, especially toes and nice smelly feet.’

‘W-w-what’s a Whivick?’ stuttered Dylan. His heart was pounding like a drum.

‘Nasty, slimy creatures with purple tongues that lash out in a flash...’

‘And that’s what’s got Emily?’

‘They’ll keep her alive for a while but we’re running out of time.’ The soldier raised the sword above his head. A silvery glow appeared at the tip. ‘Stay close. The queen will be in the deepest cavern. And keep your ears open. We don’t want anything creeping up behind us.’

‘Oh great...’ muttered Dylan, really wishing he had a shining sword as well.

5

Into The Darkness

It smelt almost pleasant at first; memories of bonfires and woodlands on a wet autumn day, mingled with the scent of the soil when he'd planted his first sunflower seeds. The tunnel was low and narrow as they walked, but it quickly widened as the path wound its way into the earth. It didn't help that huge branches jutted into the tunnel, twisting in every direction. It took a little while for Dylan to realise they weren't branches at all, but the roots of the tree.

The further in they went, the more difficult it became. Eerie creaks and groans echoed around them. Dylan kept checking over his shoulder, convinced they were about to be attacked. With every metre they travelled a horrible reeking stench grew stronger and stronger. It was even worse than the pongy cabbage in the school canteen.

The soldier kept calling for him to go faster. Soon, the muscles in his legs burned, and his side ached. Then, quite suddenly, the light from the sword disappeared behind an enormous tree root.

'Help! Don't leave me!' Dylan yelled. 'Come back...'

It was a whole ten terrifying seconds before the silvery light flashed in the darkness. Dylan didn't hesitate. Ignoring the pains in his side he ran as fast as his legs would go.

'We'll rest here, but just for a short while,' said the soldier, pulling a breathless Dylan under an overhanging root.

It took a few moments until Dylan could say anything at all. 'What's that weird noise?' he finally asked as another groaning creak echoed through the tunnels.

'When the tree sways, the roots move as well. You'll get used to it, eventually.'

Not in a zillion years, thought Dylan. He peered up at the soldier beside him. The hand holding the sword looked exactly like his, a human one. Everything about him looked so normal. 'What are you?' asked Dylan. 'I mean, do you have a name or...'

'Sergeant Archibald Dickinson, but you can call me Archie, or Sarge, I answer to either.'

'Are you a...' Dylan wanted to say toy but that just sounded wrong. 'Are you a wizard?' he said instead.

Archie laughed. 'Not exactly. I'm a soldier, although I have been around for a while.'

'So, do you know why those Whivick things took my sister?' asked Dylan.

'The queen must need a new body. If she can use a human one instead of another Whivick, she'll become very powerful.'

'*What?!*' gasped Dylan, far too loudly. From the darkness came an ominous clicking that quickly grew louder. It didn't sound friendly.

'Ssh...' hissed Archie and tugged him further under the overhang. They were only just in time. Dylan caught a glimpse of something huge, black and shiny as it scuttled to the tree-root where they were hiding.

He held his breath, his back pressed tight against the root, as two massive pincers began clicking and snapping right next to them.

The creature raised its head as if it was sniffing the air. The next second, a huge pincer was right in front of Dylan's face. He squeezed his eyes shut, waiting for the bite.

Bang! Crash! Clatter, clatter, clatter...

It sounded like the tunnel was collapsing. Startled, Dylan blinked open his eyes. The creature was scuttling away.

'That was an Earwig,' whispered Archie. 'The Whivicks made them bigger so they could use them as guards. I threw a stone to distract it. Fortunately, their eyesight is awful and they're not the cleverest of creatures.'

'S-sorry,' Dylan stuttered. 'I'll try and be quieter.' But Archie wasn't listening. Something else was coming. A cold finger of fear tickled Dylan's throat. It was a terrible sound, like an army of feet was racing towards them. 'What are we going to do, Archie? They're sure to spot us!'

Far from looking worried, the sergeant was smiling. 'We'll let the first one go and grab the second,' he whispered. 'Just follow me and do exactly what I do.'

He didn't have time to argue because Archie was already moving. Dylan glanced back up the tunnel and almost screamed. Something huge was scuttling towards them on dozens of feet. It glowed with a greeny blue haze that made it look even bigger.

'Is that a giant centipede?' gasped Dylan.

'Quiet,' warned Archie. 'They won't mean to hurt us but I don't fancy being trampled under all those feet. We let the first one run past, but the second won't be far behind. Get ready to jump.'

Before Dylan had time to think, the sergeant was running alongside the odd-looking creature. He jumped, caught hold of the first segment and swung his leg up and over its back.

It was either do the same or be left alone in the dark. Dylan took a running jump, landing with a bang on the very last segment. 'Oh – Help!' he cried, as the creature bucked, hard. Dylan went flying into the air, landing with a wallop further up the centipede's back. Again, the creature bucked. '*Help meee*,' he yelled, as again he headed towards the ceiling. He was sure he was going to end up under the creature's legs.

Archie's strong arm reached out and pulled him down. 'Hang on to the groove between the segments and don't let go,' he ordered.

It was like trying to ride a bucking bronco, but gradually the creature got used to the extra weight. Dylan even managed to sit up a little. The centipede certainly made light work of the twisting roots, running up and over them without any effort.

Dylan was just beginning to secretly enjoy the ride when Archie looked back over his shoulder and called: 'When I say jump you need to get off...Okay, now jump!'

As Dylan swung his leg over, he tried not to think about the hard floor. It rushed up to meet him, and he landed with a thump, rolling over and over. Mouth full of dust and grit, he stopped at last with a bump against a twisted root. A moment later, the sergeant crawled up beside him, a finger to his lips. All around them was a dirty red glow. The stink was worse than ever.

Carefully, Archie peered through a gap in the root and then waved Dylan to his side. Dylan had to stifle a cry.

Just a few feet away were the ugliest, strangest creatures he had ever encountered.

The Whivicks were covered in scabby yellow scales. Dark green jagged thorns ran down the centre of their backs. A snaking, purple tongue flashed in and out of their gaping mouths. They were prancing and dancing around, chanting something, which sounded a lot like '*Greeble, deeble, ummble, hissss.*' They danced about on two short hairy legs, waving hairy arms above their heads, whilst a thick green gunk oozed from their nostrils. Everywhere Dylan looked was covered in slippery slime. But that wasn't the worst of it.

In the centre of everything was a huge cauldron. It bubbled and hissed, sending up a purple haze. Two of the disgusting Whivicks were dragging someone towards it; someone who kicked and struggled as hard as they could.

Dylan gasped in horror. It was Emily!

6

Emily's Nightmare Journey

Emily knew she was in trouble as soon as she had seen the green light. One moment she had been standing up to her ankles in snow, and the next she was trapped in a weird green bubble. She'd tried shouting and hammering on the slimy walls, but Dylan hadn't heard a thing, he'd just carried on walking. Then *WHOOSH*, the world was spinning around and around. *SLAM*! She was flat on the floor, with a mouthful of snow.

Something slimy and horrible had grabbed at her arms and legs. She'd kicked and fought as hard as she could. There had been one satisfying crack and a loud yelp as her foot struck something hard, but whatever had caught her, there were just too many of them.

'Urgh! Get off me!' She'd yelled, desperate to get away from the revolting creatures. But they'd just laughed, pulling the ropes around her wrists even tighter.

'Walk!' the tallest had ordered, yanking her roughly to her feet. 'If you don't, I'll eat your toesies.' He'd drooled a little, staring hungrily down at her wellington boots. 'Our queen won't mind if I have a little nibble.'

Emily's toes had curled up tight. In the distance, she'd spotted the huge figure of Dylan. 'What have you done to me?' she'd wailed. But the creatures didn't answer. They had just pushed and pulled her towards a shimmering green hole that appeared at the foot of the towering oak.

'Hurry,' hissed the leader, and before Emily had time to wonder, two of the Whivicks had picked her up and almost thrown her inside the dank hole. She caught one last glimpse of Dylan just as he went sliding and tumbling into the snow castle.

'Where are you taking me?' she'd demanded, trying to sound brave.

'You have something the queen wants, human,' the leader had cackled.

'W-w-what's that?' stuttered Emily, not sure she really wanted to know.

'Just your body. It should only hurt for the first few hours, and then you won't remember a thing.' The leader had raised his hand to cut off the cruel cackle of laughter from the other creatures and begun to chant. *'Himble, sssimble deeble deee...'* As the words grew louder the opening in the tree closed with a grinding thud.

Emily had to bite back a scream. She hated the dark. The eerie green light wasn't much help.

'Move or we'll make you,' hissed their leader.

It had been horrible, being pushed and shoved. Emily had tried her hardest to stay on her feet but it had been really difficult with her hands tied behind her back.

'Get up!' the leader had roared after she'd fallen to the floor for about the tenth time.

'If you untied my hands I wouldn't keep falling over!' she'd shouted back. It had to be the worst nightmare ever, she'd thought misera-bly, but the bruises on her knees felt real enough.

'Cut her ropes,' the leader had finally ordered, fed up with the delays. 'But if you try and run, I'm going to have a toe.' His snaking purple tongue had lashed out, tickling her cheek.

The creatures had pushed and tugged her up and over the huge gnarled roots that spiralled across their path. A few times she'd glanced back along the tunnel, tempted to make a run for it, but there had been too many evil eyes flickering in the darkness.

As they'd travelled further down the endless tunnel, a strange red glow had appeared in the distance. Soft at first, it soon became brighter and the stink almost unbearable. They'd stopped once again beside an enormous twisting tree root.

'On the other side of this our queen is waiting,' the leader had cackled.

The creatures had grabbed hold of her, pushing and shoving her up the side of the root, until she'd found herself sitting astride the very top. In front of her, more of the weird creatures had been dancing around a large pot that hissed and bubbled. Then she had glanced back the other way and had almost fallen off the root in fright. A huge creature was racing down the tunnel towards them. It was hard to make out, but she was sure there was something riding on its back; something wearing a bright yellow bobble hat.

'Get down here,' the leader had ordered, grabbing her leg so she slid with a bump to the floor.

That had to be Dylan; no one else would've worn such a ridiculous hat. Emily had scrambled to her feet and had then done something she'd never thought herself capable of.

'Hi-yah!' she'd roared as loudly as she could. Kicking out at the creature to her left, she'd spun around, pushing over the one to her right. Down they'd toppled like skittles. The fallen Whivicks rocked on their backs, kicking their hairy legs in despair. They couldn't get back up! Others had leapt forwards, but she'd spun fast, kicking and jabbing. They'd kept fall-

ing, one on top of the other. It would've been funny if she hadn't been so scared.

It was the slimy, slippery floor that finally caught her out. With an anguished cry of 'Help!' Emily started to slide. Arms whirling, out of control, she had slid faster and faster, until she had landed right at the feet of the queen with a *splat*.

The wizened old creature had scales of a dull red instead of yellow. She wore a pearly coloured cloak, all twisted and knotted together like it was made from the finest spider's web.

'Purr-fect,' snarled the queen, her green eyes glinting. 'Soon I will be all powerful.' Her evil laughter had echoed around the chamber. 'Tie her to the stake,' she'd ordered. 'Time is running out.'

7

Who Is Saving Who?

As Dylan crouched beside the sergeant in the shadow of the root, he could hardly keep still. 'We've got to do something before those Whivicks boil her up.'

'We wait until they start the chant,' whispered Archie.

Dylan was about to argue when something heavy nudged him in the back. He froze, hardly daring to breathe. There was another push followed by a funny sort of snort. He risked a quick peep. 'Hey, stop that,' Dylan hissed. The centipede had its head down, ready to butt again. Its beady eyes gleamed pink in the red glow.

'I told you, it's harmless, apart from those feet,' whispered Archie. 'I think it must like you.'

It was a bit like being leant on by a pony or a massive dog. Dylan tried to push it away but the centipede kept nudging its head against the pocket of his coat. Then it dawned on him.

'I bet it can smell my biscuit, Archie.' But the sergeant wasn't listening; he was too busy watching the Whivicks. Dylan dug out a few of the broken crumbs and scattered them on the ground. He could've sworn the centipede began to purr.

'Get ready.' Archie's warning was fierce. 'And take this.' The soldier had ripped off a long piece of root. 'Beware of the venom on their tongues and in their blood. If any gets in your eyes you won't be able to move.' Dylan pushed up his glasses, trying to pretend he wasn't scared. 'We will aim for their legs and knock them over. They have a real problem getting back to their feet,' Archie explained. With a flash of silver, the sword was out of its sheath. 'Forwards,' he urged and began to climb the side of the root.

When Dylan finally reached the top he could see the Whivick queen below, crouched over a seething cauldron. His sister had been tied to a stake at the side. Emily's lips were moving but it was impossible to hear what she was saying.

As they slid silently down the other side, the chants of the Whivicks grew louder and the dancing more frantic. Everywhere Dylan looked, the ugly creatures were whirling around in a frenzied jig. Suddenly, from the bubbling, hissing brew in the cauldron, a stream of purple liquid shot out.

The queen rose to her full height and threw off the pearly robe. ‘Now – just a single bite of that tasty little toe and then into the pot with the rest of you...’ She waved two of the Whivicks towards her.

‘No!’ yelled Emily, as slimy hands reached to pull off her boots. The first kick sent one Whivick flying several feet into the air; another tumbled over and over. Emily jiggled and wriggled, kicked and fought but Dylan could see her strength was fading.

No one had spotted Dylan and the sergeant creeping up. All eyes were fixed on their queen. With a *CRACK*, the sergeant’s sword smashed into the first group. Whivicks flew off in all directions, bouncing into walls and each other.

Dylan didn’t hang about. ‘Take *that!*’ he yelled, and began whacking at their legs.

Whivicks went tumbling and sprawling, sliding across the slimy floor.

A piercing scream echoed across the chamber. The queen had managed to pull off one of Emily's boots. Sharp teeth bared, she was about to take a bite.

'Archie...do something!' Dylan cried.

A sword spun through the air. There was a yelp followed by a loud splash as the hilt knocked the queen straight into the bubbling cauldron. Archie ran forwards, pulled out the sword from the seething mess and slashed at Emily's ropes.

But even as Dylan let out a roar of triumph, he heard a terrible hissing cackle. A crowd of furious Whivicks was advancing on him, edging him back towards that bubbling cauldron. He was trapped!

'You'll do,' snarled the tallest. 'We'll have a king instead of a queen.'

With a flash of silver, Archie and Emily were suddenly at his side. The sergeant's sword swirled so fast it was almost a blur.

'Keep back to back,' Archie yelled. 'We must stay together.'

Dylan's shoulders ached from the effort as he thumped hard at the Whivick's legs. As soon as one fell down, another sprang forward to take its place. Risking a quick glance towards the dark tunnel, his heart sank. Dozens more Whivicks blocked their escape. There was no way out.

It was then that he had a sudden brilliant idea...or at least it would be if he could get a hand into his pocket. Dylan got in one almighty whack with his stick. The large Whivick in front of him tumbled into another and, just like skittles, knocked three more down.

Seizing his moment, Dylan dug out a biscuit from his pocket. The first lump went whizzing over the Whivick's heads, right over the top of the tree root. He threw several more pieces. Each time the lumps of biscuit landed just a little bit closer.

Behind him, his sister kept kicking and pushing, and the sergeant's sword didn't waiver, but Dylan knew they couldn't keep going forever.

Just as he was beginning to lose hope, it happened; a flurry of cries, roars of pain, and the rhythmic *thumpty thump* of legs.

‘What is it now?’ groaned Emily.

‘That’s our transport out of here,’ said Dylan, grinning in relief.

‘Take your sister and show her what to do,’ ordered Archie. ‘I’ll watch your backs.’

Grabbing Emily’s hand, Dylan dodged between the confused creatures, straight towards the oncoming centipede. The sergeant charged, beating away the angry Whivicks that were hitting the poor insect, trying to make it flee.

‘Jump up and hang on to one of the ridges on its back,’ called Dylan. ‘It bucks sometimes, so be careful.’

'Are you serious?' Emily spluttered.

'Yes. Now get on!'

He heard his sister grumble as she swung up behind him, and then squeal as the centipede began to move. They'd almost reached the tree root when Dylan glanced back over his shoulder. 'We have to go back,' he yelled. 'I'm not leaving Archie...'

The sergeant was surrounded. All Dylan could see was the flashing sword as it disappeared beneath a horde of slathering slimy Whivicks.

8

Feathers

Dylan leant over, grabbed the thin whiskers on one side of the insect's face and gently tugged. The centipede did a strange sort of shiver, which rippled all the way down its back, and turned. Dylan dug in his heels. 'Hold on tight to the ridge,' he warned. 'This could get hairy.'

He clung on, hoping Emily would manage. He could hear her bouncing up and down and groaning but he didn't dare to look around. The centipede arrived in the cavern with a clatter. Head down, it gave an angry snort and ran straight at the Whivicks, scattering them. They tried running left and right; some even tried climbing the walls, desperate to avoid the charging feet.

Clinging on with one arm, Dylan held out his other for the sergeant, trying desperately hard not to fall. With a last swing of his sword, Archie grabbed Dylan's arm and leapt.

Now there were three astride one very annoyed centipede!

'Get us out of here,' Archie yelled, kicking out at a desperate Whivick who was pulling at his legs.

From the cauldron came a terrible, stomach-churning bellow of rage. The old queen clambered out from the smoking liquid, purple gloop sliding from her hair and nostrils.

'*Stop them!*' she screamed, pointing a long bony finger.

Dylan gave a firm tug on the centipede's whiskers and a dig in its side. 'You'd better hold on,' he yelled, as the now furious centipede turned sharply, knocking Whivicks in every direction.

In three strides it was up and over the tree root and racing away down the tunnel, running faster than it had ever run in its life. From behind came a roar of fury. The Whivicks weren't quick to give up, but their grunts and yells soon faded as the centipede sped away.

'Slow him down a little. He can't keep up this pace,' Archie shouted in Dylan's ear. 'We need to keep him going for as long as we can.'

Dylan leant back, lifting his legs away from the creature's side. Sure enough, they began to slow. 'Clever centipede,' Dylan called. 'I promise I'll give you the rest of the biscuit as soon as we stop.' He shouted over his shoulder. 'Are you all right Emily?' She was clinging on and looked grim but at least she wasn't bumping around anymore.

'I just want to get out of here,' she called back.

'Not far now,' Archie said. 'Once we're over the next big root we'll need to jump off.'

It was a good thing too, thought Dylan. The centipede was already tiring. It managed to scramble over the final root but came to a juddering halt on the other side. They all slid off. Dylan patted the exhausted centipede's side fondly.

'Stay here, I need to find the opening,' said Archie. He began tapping the walls of the tunnel, his ear to the wood.

'Why are these centipedes so big?' asked Dylan. He pulled out a few more bits of biscuit. The centipede instantly raised its head and sniffed.

'The Whivicks enchanted them,' Archie explained. 'They use them for food. Now be quiet and let me listen.'

'But that's not fair. It saved us.' Emily began to stroke the creature's cheek.

'Yeah, we can't just let them eat it,' said Dylan. 'Can't you do something, Archie?'

Archie sighed. 'I suppose there is one thing I can do. Step away,' he ordered. Raising his sword, he waved it three times along the centipede's back. There was a flash, a whizz and then…

'Where's it gone?' asked Dylan, glancing around.

'Try looking down,' said the soldier and turned back to the tunnel walls.

A normal-sized centipede scuttled away, to hide beneath a pile of loose earth.

'Wow,' Emily murmured, impressed.

'Finally, I've found it.' Archie's triumphant cry was followed by a crack of silvery light, which quickly widened into a hole.

'Uh-oh...' hissed Dylan. 'I can hear them coming.' Sure enough, the yells and grunts were getting steadily louder.

'Outside, now,' ordered Archie.

The night air was cool and fresh, even the cold snow felt good. With a grating crack, the hole snapped shut, but Archie still looked concerned.

'We're running out of time and they can still get out.' He broke off two twigs from a fallen branch. 'Keep hitting this part of the tree with these, as hard as you can. The vibrations should slow them down.' He whacked one of the twigs against the trunk to show them what he meant.

'Can't you just make us bigger?' pleaded Emily.

'I used too much magic holding off those Whivicks. If I try and fail, the Whivicks will win. Now, keep using those sticks. I'm going to get us some help.'

'What's he doing?' hissed Emily as Archie began climbing the huge oak. Dylan shook his head. He had no idea. Archie's tiny feet found footholds in the rough bark easily enough and he was soon out of sight.

'*Look out!*' warned Emily. A green glow had started to form a new doorway. They began hitting the tree trunk hard. *Thwack, thwack.*

They kept going until Dylan thought his arms were going to fall off. At least the glow wasn't getting any brighter.

'He'd better hurry up,' panted Emily. 'I can't do this for much longer.'

There was a sudden rush of wind and a rustling sound. Not daring to stop, Dylan glanced over his shoulder and almost toppled with fright. An enormous owl was sat blinking at them. Its huge eyes were like dark pools of water. Emily's eyes were almost as large, as she stared back in panic.

'The door!' shouted Dylan; the green was much brighter. Archie sprang to their side. With an almighty heave, he whacked the tree with his sword. The green light faded to little more than a glimmer.

'He's agreed to carry us, but we must move quickly. The clock will soon be chiming.'

'The owl?' Dylan couldn't believe it. Earlier it had wanted him for supper, and now he was supposed to just —

Before Dylan could complete his train of thought, Archie picked him up and threw him onto the owl's feathery back. Emily followed moments later. 'Hold gently to his feathers,' said Archie, and jumped up behind them. 'He flies smoothly, but he might object if you pull out his coat.'

With a *whish* and a *swish,* the owl began flapping its huge wings. For a moment it was running along the ground, and then with a jolt they rose into the night sky.

‘Oh wow...I am so going to learn to be a pilot,’ called Emily, as the wind whipped around them.

‘Me too,’ shouted Dylan, gazing down at the ice-covered pond.

A distance ominous sound rang out.

Ding Dong Ding Dong, Ding Dong Ding Dong –

DONG! went the first chime.

‘Oh no, the window is closed!’ yelled Dylan, staring at the fast approaching house.

DONG!

‘We’ll never make it,’ called Emily.

DONG!

The owl slowed a little, allowing two more DONGS to chime. There were only seconds left. The soldier raised his sword just as the sixth chime rang out.

DONG!

Dylan and Emily cheered as the window slid up to the sound of chime number seven.

DONG!

The owl slowed again, swooping a little as it curved its wings. Dylan closed his eyes, convinced they would hit the side of the house.

DONG!

‘What happens if we don’t make it?’ yelled Emily.

DONG!

The owl's talons scraped on the edge of the windowsill, balancing precariously.

DONG!

'You really don't want to know,' yelled Archie.

DONG!

He grabbed them and jumped, sending them rolling onto the floor.

DONG!!!

The world went topsy-turvy. It was like everything was whizzing around inside Dylan's mother's blender, being sliced and diced at the same time. Round and down, up and in. A roaring noise tore through Dylan's head, like a train going through a tunnel.

'*Dylan?* Dylan, are you all right?'

He blinked hard, for a moment unsure where he was. There was his bed, and he could see his truck. It was just a normal-sized toy, so he must be back to full size.

'That was cutting it close,' said a tinny voice. Dylan turned his head; Sergeant Archibald Dickinson was still toy-sized. 'You must close and lock your window. We won this battle, but there are other things abroad and the magic seems strong tonight.'

Dylan blinked again, wondering why everything looked hazy. His glasses were covered with a horrible gooey green mess. Though his knees felt like jelly, he hurried to the window and pulled it shut. The latch was stiff but he managed to push it across.

'What do you mean by *"other things"?'* asked Emily. She sat up, rubbing her head.

'Once the clock strikes one, you'll be safe enough. Just make sure you keep your bedroom window locked at night, at least until the new moon.'

'But Archie,' Dylan said, 'do you go back to just being a toy?'

'I was never a toy,' said Archie, brushing off his uniform. 'I need to get back to my friends. I think it's time we had a talk with old Snifflebit. There's more going on than I bargained for.'

'What's a Snifflebit?' asked Emily. But Archie was already marching towards the door.

'Sergeant Archie, are those other figures magic as well?' asked Dylan as they hurried after him.

'The party is finishing. Your parents will be coming to check on you soon,' was all Archie said.

With a sigh, Dylan opened the door. 'I am really sorry about the catapult,' he muttered.

'Don't mention it,' grumbled Archie. 'It's not the first time it's happened to me.' He gave a piercing whistle. Next moment a thin rope slithered down from the shelf. Emily and Dylan watched open-mouthed as the camouflaged figure knelt and deftly hoisted Archie up until he was standing beside him. From the hallway below came the sound of their parent's voices. They were already saying goodbye to friends. Dylan guessed they only had minutes before they would be up.

'I don't know how to thank you,' whispered Emily.

'Do not go out into that garden at night for any reason. Do you promise?' said Archie, now at eye level.

'Promise,' they whispered together.

'And don't talk about this to anyone. It isn't safe,' he warned.

They heard the front door closing. There wasn't time to say anything else. Rushing back into the bedroom, they managed to pull off coats, hat and boots and stuffed them under Emily's bed. Dylan remembered to slip his gunky glasses under his pillow, just before the bedroom door opened.

'I can't believe they managed to sleep through all that noise,' murmured their father.

'Nor me. I'm glad we let them stay, despite Dad trying to put us off,' said their mother.

'It just wouldn't be right being here without them,' he whispered back. The door closed.

Dylan lay blinking up at the shadowy ceiling. His heart was still racing. 'Did you hear that?' he whispered. 'Why doesn't Grandad like us being here?'

‘Of course he does,’ insisted Emily. ‘He must have thought the party would keep us awake.’

‘Well it did,’ whispered Dylan.

‘Dylan,’ she murmured. ‘Did all that really happen? Those creatures and everything?’

‘Pinch yourself,’ suggested Dylan. ‘If it hurts then you know it was for real.’

‘That makes no sense at all,’ Emily said, beginning to sound like his usual grumpy sister.

‘Well, there’s all that green stuff on my glasses,’ said Dylan, taking them out from under his pillow.

‘I’m going to sleep,’ Emily whispered. ‘I don’t want to think about those ugly things anymore.’ Without another word, she pulled the duvet up over her head.

9

Did It Really Happen?

It was the wintery sunlight streaming in through the window that woke Dylan. He stretched, wondering why his legs and arms ached so much. Memory flooded back. He pushed on his glasses; everything was still blurry.

'Emily, are you awake?'

'Am now,' she moaned.

'My glasses, they're all covered in green gunk.' He held them up to the light for her to see. They stared at each other for a long moment.

'We'd better get our coats and stuff back downstairs before Mum sees,' she whispered.

While Dylan cleaned his glasses, Emily knelt down to pull out the wellingtons and coats from under her bed. 'They've gone...' she hissed.

'What?' said Dylan. 'Mum must've spotted them.'

'But I'd have heard her, I'm positive,' said Emily. 'We need to get downstairs and check.'

When they stepped out into the hallway they discovered the three lead figures had disappeared from the shelf.

'I bet they're back in Grandad's study,' Dylan said. They crept down the small staircase to the back door. Hanging from the pegs were their coats and hat, their wellingtons stood neatly in a row. Dylan pushed his hand into his coat pocket and shivered. 'Look,' he whispered. 'Crumbs from those biscuits...'

Their mother was already at the kitchen table sipping a hot drink. She looked up from the paper she was reading and smiled. Apart from looking tired she didn't look cross at all. 'I thought I heard you about. I've just put some porridge on, it won't be long. Thanks for being so good last night. I know we made quite a lot of noise.' She yawned. 'Your dad should be down in a minute. Would you like some juice?'

They ate in silence, still not sure what to make of everything.

'Are you two feeling all right?' asked their father, eyeing the quiet pair.

Dylan nodded. He wanted desperately to ask if he knew about Archie the soldier, or if he'd ever heard of a Snifflebit, but remembered the sergeant's warning and kept quiet.

'Did you enjoy the party, Dad?' Emily asked, trying to fill the awkward silence.

'I did, thank you. I even saved you some trifle. I thought we could take your sleds up to the top field later. I just need to help your mum clear up a bit first.'

'That would be great,' said Dylan.

They had to walk past the snow castle to reach the small gate and the road beyond. Dylan felt odd when he saw the hole in the turret where the sergeant had landed.

'Looks as if a fox has had a go at your castle,' said his father, pointing to the side where Dylan had landed with a bump.

'And I can see tiny footprints over by the oak,' murmured Dylan, as he followed Emily out into the lane.

'It's just too weird,' she whispered.

It was a good ten-minute walk to the steep sloping field. Wrapped up warmly, they carried the bright red sleds under their arms.

'Dad, how long has Grandad lived in this house?' asked Dylan as they trudged through the snow.

'Ever since he was born,' his dad explained. 'As far as I know, several of your great grandfather's did as well.'

'It's a funny sort of place,' said Dylan, and almost fell over as Emily gave him a hard nudge. 'Sort of spooky I mean. Er…' He was beginning to wish he hadn't said anything.

'It's a bit strange I suppose, and the creaking floorboards and doors don't help,' said his father. 'But I've always felt safe here and I know your mum loves it.' He smiled down at them. 'She'd move back here tomorrow if she could.'

'So why don't we?' asked Emily.

'It takes a lot of money to keep the place warm and so much needs repairing. And for some reason your grandfather wasn't that keen.' He pointed ahead to the field. Several other children were already making good use of the steep slopes. 'Come on, let's go and join the fun,' he said, and marched away without another word.

'Why wouldn't Grandad want us to live here?' muttered Dylan.

'Who would want to live with you if they didn't have to?' Emily teased. 'Come on, I want to do some sledding.'

Dylan looked anxiously over his shoulder. 'Don't you think we should tell him what happened?'

'No way. He'd think we were mad.'

'It's cool though, knowing there's magic and stuff,' said Dylan, as he trudged along behind her. 'Especially riding a centipede, that was way neat.'

'If you say so,' said Emily, sounding unconvinced. 'I'm beginning to think it was some sort of dream.'

'How can you say that?' Dylan spluttered. 'There's the snow castle where I fell into the side, and what about those footprints near the tree?'

'Could have been a fox or a bird,' she insisted. 'Anyway, what about our coats and stuff? I didn't take them back and I know you didn't.'

'What about that gunky stuff on my glasses and the biscuit crumbs in my pockets?' Dylan demanded. 'Those Whivick things were definitely for real.'

'I never ever want to see another ugly Whivick as long as I live,' Emily hissed, and with that she flounced off, her head held high.

Neither did he, thought Dylan as he watched her go.

But he had a horrible feeling last night's adventure was only the beginning...

About The Author

Born in Newport, South Wales, I have lived in many different parts of the country and am currently to be found roosting near Pontefract, West Yorkshire.

Also, a writer of children's short stories and poems, I am working on the second book in the Oozing magic series, 'Deep Waters.'

For those who enjoy a longer read, I have also written a fast-paced adventure story, 'A Fistful of Feathers' for 10-13-year old's. The second book in this series, 'Flight or Fight,' is to be published very shortly.

With frequent stops for fruit cake, ginger biscuits, chocolate cake, and the occasional apple, the next year promises to be *very* busy.

As this book is one of millions to choose from, I'm honoured that it was the one you picked up. It's great that there is so much choice, but it also means authors rely on readers sharing their thoughts about the book they've just read with their friends.

You can do this online, by posting a review on Amazon, or mentioning it in relevant discussions. I'd also be hugely grateful if you could share a link to it on your social media platforms, so other readers can find it and enjoy it, too.

Remember: Authors are nothing without their readers!

Why not leave me a message on my Facebook page?
www.facebook.com/LindaJonesukAuthor

Now read on and enjoy the short extract from A Fistful Of Feathers –

He's running - but danger lurks in every shadow!

An Introduction To A Fistful Of Feathers

It's bad enough being thirteen. Not having a family, and never living anywhere longer than a few months... now that's pretty rough. But what really stinks is living with a massive lump on your neck that just keeps growing!

Jo, part of an illegal experiment that could cost him his life, decides to go on the run, so the sinister Dr Bowden can't perform the 'final examination'. No one has *ever* survived that experience.

He finally finds safety and true friendship amongst a group of people who don't see him as a freak.

But lurking in the shadows, Bowden's men are waiting, ready to pounce. Jo has to make a choice: submit to Bowden and be hauled back to that creepy clinic, or expose his secret to save them all – and risk losing the only friends he's ever known.

Available in print and an e-book on Amazon -
ISBN 978-1-9993248-1-0

Chapter 1: The Clinic

Jo hated going to the clinic. The journey there was bad enough, mile after mile of mind-numbing boredom. When they finally arrived, the driver, strode beside him down the long corridor, his heels clipping sharply on the cold tiles. Then came the same menacing warning as he pushed open the waiting room door.

'You stay put, Ranson, or else...'

This visit was no different. Jo counted the driver's steps as he walked away; he waited for the swish of the heavy doors and that final click. It meant freedom, of sorts. Cautiously, Jo edged his way out of the small waiting room and did his best to glance back up the now-silent corridor. It wasn't easy, the huge swelling on the back of his neck made everything - other than looking at the floor - almost impossible.

The place really gave him the creeps. Each time he came, he was marched past brightly decorated rooms where other patients were allowed to wait. He had to step through those double doors, where everything turned drab and gloomy.

Whether awake or in his nightmares, the corridor never altered. The walls were the same grubby beige colour, with cracks and flaking paint as the only decoration. On the floor were eight-hundred-and-twenty-three dingy grey tiles, each with a green crescent moon at its centre. Seven of them were broken, he knew because he'd counted them loads of times. Even the smell was always the same - a bit like the school toilets on a Monday morning; it reeked of disinfectant.

It was stupid having to wait in such a poxy hole, and even worse, he was starving. All he'd managed to grab that morning were two slabs of bread and cheese. He studied the doors again, picturing what was on the other side. The vending machine wasn't far. He passed it every time he came, so he knew it was packed full: drinks, crisps, sandwiches, chocolates bars.

It was tempting, and he had money hidden in the waistband of his trousers. The driver checked his pockets every time he picked him up, but so far, he'd not found this emergency fund.

Jo's pulse quickened. The thought of filling his aching stomach spurred him on. Eleven strides, that's all it would take to reach those doors. His feet were already moving. He could be there and back in two minutes. Just three more steps. This time, he wouldn't get caught. He'd stuff his pockets full and...

Jo stopped dead, his heart pounding. Through the small frosted pane of glass in the door, the outline of the driver's hat was just visible. He must be talking to someone right outside.

It was like he was nine years-old all over again. That time, he'd made it all the way to the vending machine. He remembered putting in his money. The carton of juice, suspended, ready to fall. He stretched out a hand ready to pick it up and then...

'Gotcha...' Terrified, he was rooted to the spot. The driver's shadow had loomed over him, like a scary monster from a horror film. 'You'll be lucky to sit down this side of Christmas,' he'd hissed. 'Start walking.' The driver marched him straight back. Jo bore slap marks on his legs for days.

His heart still thudding, Jo turned back; it just wasn't worth the risk. Pushing his thick, sandy-coloured hair from his eyes, he kept his gaze fixed on the tiles, away from the other end of the corridor and the 'torture chamber'. He'd see that place soon enough. A few minutes later, a nurse in a blue uniform pushed through the doors. For a moment, Jo's spirits lifted. If it was Maggie, his favourite nurse, she wouldn't mind fetching him something from the machine. But it wasn't. He'd never seen this nurse before, and if she mentioned his request to the driver, Jo could say goodbye to his money.

Fed up, he waited for her to disappear before checking the clock in the room opposite. It was only quarter-past eleven. Doctor Bowden never got to the clinic before midday. He rummaged through the pile of magazines on the small table but they were all old copies. More cheesed off than ever, he slouched back in his seat.

'I hate this stinking place!' He kicked out at an unoffending chair so hard that it crashed into the wall. Chips of plaster puffed into the air like confetti. Seconds later, footsteps clicked rapidly down the corridor. He didn't care anymore if he got into trouble.

'Are you alright?' Concerned, the nurse stood at the door.

'Fine. I…tripped,' he lied, rattling the plastic chair back into place.

'Well, if you do want me, press the buzzer. I'm just having a quick bite before I start in the other clinic.' She walked off.

'Lucky you,' muttered Jo. His stomach growled noisily at the thought of food.

He waited until he couldn't hear the nurse's footsteps then pushed the small table under the window. Every visit he did the same thing. Scrambling on top, he pulled one of the plastic chairs up after him. It was dangerous, standing on the wobbly chair on top of the table, but it was the only way to see outside. The window was locked, of course. In the distance, he could just make out the edges of another building. It seemed to be empty. Even when they passed it in the car, he never saw anyone near it, not that he could see much. The tinted windows and the driver's shoulders usually obscured most of the car's windscreen.

'What are you doing, Jo?'

'WHOA!' The chair began to rock violently. He grabbed the windowsill, his heart thumping like a drum. 'Amy!' A curious face peered up at him. 'Why creep up on me like that?' He didn't mean to sound so cross. Her smile disappeared in a flash.

'I wasn't. Sorry,' she mumbled

'It's okay, you just startled me. I thought you were the driver.'

'Oh, him!' She shuddered. 'What were you doing?'

'Just looking. I was hoping the window was open so I could do a runner.' He said it with a smile, but he meant every word. 'Are you okay?' he asked her, as he climbed down. The swelling on her neck wasn't as big as his, but he could see it had grown from the last time they'd met. Even with her shoulder length hair it was obvious.

She bowed her head letting her hair cover her face. 'Suppose,' she shrugged. 'I'm hungry. I've been here for hours already. I've been doing those exercises like you showed me though and they've helped loosen me up lots.' She checked over her shoulder. 'It's been hard, keeping it secret when I do them, especially as they moved me to another family last week. It's not fair, Jo. I'd only just got sorted from the last move.'

He could tell by her sad eyes that it had not been a good move. He had only met Amy a year ago. Until then, he'd been convinced that he was the only one in the whole world with such a swelling on his neck. Even more shocking, Amy swore that she'd seen at least two other teenagers with the same 'thing'.

'Are you still on that farm, with those Bigwells?' she asked

'I am.' Jo smiled. 'It's almost a year now and Doc Bowden still hasn't found out I'm going to that school.'

'Does Bert Bigwell still make you do all the farm work?' Amy asked.

'Yeah, but I don't mind.' He grinned. 'Every time I come to the clinic, he panics. He thinks I'll tell the doc about all the stuff I have to do around the farm. But I'm not going to say a word, as long as I can carry on going to school.'

'Well, I think you were really brave standing up to Bigwell,' she said. 'And I can't believe you got one over on the Doc.'

'I just hope it stays that way.'

'Me too.' Amy gave a heartfelt sigh. 'It's going to be my birthday next week, I'll be eleven.' There was no excitement in her voice. Jo noticed how pale her cheeks were and wondered how bad things had become.

'Well, happy birthday from me,' he said, as cheerfully as he could. 'Mine isn't until April, then I'll be fourteen. I'll probably spend it with the pigs. They're always good for a laugh.' Amy only managed a feeble smile.

'Tell you what, how about we play some stupid games?' he suggested 'Anything you like, your choice.'

It didn't take much to bring Amy's sparkle back. 'You're so silly,' she said, twenty minutes later. 'That sounds nothing like a cockerel.'

'It's got a sore throat! Anyway, I think that makes you today's grand winner.'

'Have you got any friends at that school?' she asked him as they fell silent.

'Just the one, Dan Fraser. But he's not going to be there for much longer. He's moving away.' Just saying it made Jo's emptiness feel ten times worse.

'Oh, I'm...' Amy stopped abruptly. Her eyes grew wide. 'It's Doctor Bowden!' she mouthed.

'He'll go straight to his room, don't worry,' Jo whispered. They waited in silence until they heard his door click. 'Go, while it's clear. Jo said. 'Remember, not a word about school or the farm.'

'Promise.' She flashed him a quick smile then she was gone.

Jo sank onto one of the hard chairs, the familiar knot of anger beginning to tighten. Why was this happening to them? Why couldn't they just cut the stupid lumps off? It wasn't fair - none of it was fair. He'd get away from the

Bigwells, go to another doctor, or the police. The same thoughts ran through his head a dozen times a day. What was the point of anything? He was just useless.

By the time Doctor Bowden buzzed for him, Jo hardly had the energy to stand. Stepping out into the corridor, he glanced longingly towards the doors that lead out to freedom. He turned back toward his nightmare. It would take just nine short steps to reach Bowden's office. Nine, eight, seven...

The examination was the usual torture, except this time, Bowden didn't take any blood. Jo gritted his teeth, determined not to yelp as cold fingers prodded. He knew better than to complain. At last, Bowden barked, 'Put your shirt back on.'

Jo dared to ask a question. 'Doctor Bowden, when will it stop growing? Only, it seems to be getting so much bigger.'

'Nothing to worry about,' Bowden said, still looking down at his notes.

Jo threw caution to the wind. 'Can't you just cut it off, or do something? You have to, it isn't fair!'

Cold, dark eyes glared at Jo under thick eyebrows. He had a small, pointy beard, splattered with grey. It wagged like an angry finger when he spoke. 'It will all be over soon. That, I promise.' Bowden's words held no comfort.

'What do you mean?'

Bowden's pale lips curled into a smile that was about as warm as an ice cube. 'Just what I said. Another few months, Ranson, and it will all be over. Now, get dressed.

Printed in Great Britain
by Amazon